THE TOBERMORY CAT

BY DEBI GLIORI

BIRLINN

A long time ago,
    before you were born,
    the little Hebridean island of Mull
    was home to hundreds of cats.

Cats of all colours and clans could be found
roaming its highlands and lowlands,

FISHNISH
⚓
30KM

SALEN

CARSAIG

and it seemed
that every village
had its very own,
special kind of cat.

The people of Loch Ba
were proud to tell visitors
that there was *nothing* on earth
as soft as the woolly cats
of Loch Ba.

The Staffa boatman
swore he'd never heard
a sweeter sound
than the song of the
cats of Staffa.

The villagers
of Salen boasted that
there hadn't been
a beastie born
more sullen than
the sulky cats of Salen,

and the Fishnish
sailors said that
there wasn't a creature
alive, alive-o
could hook a haddock
like the sea-faring cats
of Fishnish.

The people of Loch Ba,
Staffa, Salen and Fishnish
were only too delighted to show
visitors round their villages
and sell them
their cat postcards

and cat t-shirts

and cat soap

and cat chocolates.

Everyone agreed that
cats were a very good thing
to bring in the visitors.

However, the little Hebridean fishing village of Tobermory
on the island of Mull was *also* home to several cats.
None of these was especially woolly or musical or sulky,
and all of them, without exception, *hated* the sea.

The Tobermory cats
liked nothing better than
catching mice, eating fish,
watching clouds,
and sleeping.
The Tobermory cats
were very *ordinary* cats,
and, sadly, nobody wanted
to visit Tobermory to see them.

In fact, what with
the famously woolly Ba-Ba Cats,
the Singing Cat Choir of Staffa,
the Snotty Cats of Salen
and the Fishing Felines of Fishnish,
hardly *anybody* bothered to visit Tobermory anymore.

This was a great shame, because it meant nobody visited its fish cafe

or its bookshop

or its beautiful
launderette

or its amazing
hardware store,
where you could find
everything you needed

ARCH BROWNS SOY

plus gold-plated reindeer,
green electric guitars,
purple fur-lined wellies
and the odd ocarina.

Without visitors,
the people of Tobermory grew desperate.
They had a meeting in the village hall.

Our fish are floundering.

Our books are mouldering.

Our launderette is folding.

Something *had* to be done. 'I know,' said a very small person, 'let's teach *our* cats how to be special.'

This was not a success.
   As anyone who has ever tried to train a cat
      will tell you, it is almost impossible
         to make a cat do anything it doesn't want to do.
   And, if you remember, all that the Tobermory cats
            wanted to do was catch mice, eat fish,
                watch clouds and sleep.

                  All except for one ginger tom.
                  He was keen, he was quick,
                     he was willing to learn.
                  'Show me,' he miaowed,
                  'how to become a special cat.'

But no amount of training
could make him woolly,
or musical, or sulky, and,
if you remember,
he *hated* the sea.

The people of Tobermory
gave up trying to train cats
and went back to work.

But the ginger tom didn't give up.

He tried to ask a visiting celebrity for advice.
'Show me,' he miaowed.
'I want to be special like you.'
But the celebrity was far too busy
being a celebrity to speak to
an ordinary cat.

But the ginger tom
still didn't give up.

read the sign
on the fish van.

'Show me,' miaowed the cat.
'I want to be special too.'
But no matter what
the cat did, the fish refused
to give up their secrets.

But the ginger cat was quick.
He was keen.
He was willing to learn.
Even if his teacher was somewhat unusual.

'Show me,' he miaowed,
over the roar
of the big yellow digger,

'SHOW ME HOW TO BE SPECIAL.'
The big yellow digger ignored the cat
and got on with digging up Main Street.

The cat miaowed louder and louder
but nobody could hear a word he said.

The ginger tom gritted his teeth.
Being special was proving to be
harder than he'd imagined.

He decided to ask his friends
for advice.

'Show me,' he miaowed. 'How do I become a special cat?'

His friends stared at him. The little dog laughed.
The cow blinked. The dish nudged the spoon and said,
'You are special already. Just be yourself.'

The ginger tom sighed.
Nobody understood.

It seemed that nobody could help him become special.

He might as well just give up trying.

With little enthusiasm,
he caught mice,

ate fish,

gazed at the clouds,

and bored himself to sleep.

The next day, there was
a huge traffic jam
in Tobermory.
Cars, bikes, vans and
even the school bus
ground to a standstill
on Main Street.
Right in the middle
of the road
lay the ginger cat,
fast asleep.
Everyone wanted
a photograph of him.
Everyone had
heard of him.

It was only a matter of time before the ginger cat's fame spread further afield. From twig, to leaf, to nest, to telegraph pole, by mouth, by mail, by phone, by email,

soon the whole island, then the mainland, and then the entire planet was a-twitter with the news of the amazing Cat of Tobermory.

Not everyone was delighted
with the news.
'I'm sure his fur is nothing special,'
said the famously woolly Ba-Ba Cats.

'A Tobermory Cat?

Where's the music in that?'
sang the Staffa Cat Choir,

while the snotty Cats of Salen
simply rolled their eyes and sneered.

And since everybody knows that cats
from Tobermory *hate* the sea,
the Fishing Felines of Fishnish
decided they had nothing
whatsoever to worry about.

And the Tobermory Cat?
Fame has not changed him.
He is still himself.

TOBER
MORY

♥ t⊙bermⓞry

He is still not sure what it means to be special. But when he thinks nobody is watching . . .

To the people of Mull who gave this book their blessing ~ this is for you

First published in 2012 by
Birlinn Limited
West Newington House, 10 Newington Road
Edinburgh EH9 1QS

ISBN: 978 1 78027 099 9

British Library Cataloguing-in-Publication Data
A catalogue record for this book is available from the British Library

Typeface 'Tom Anderson's Fiddle' designed by Debi Gliori and Martin Salisbury
Printed and bound by Proost NV, Belgium

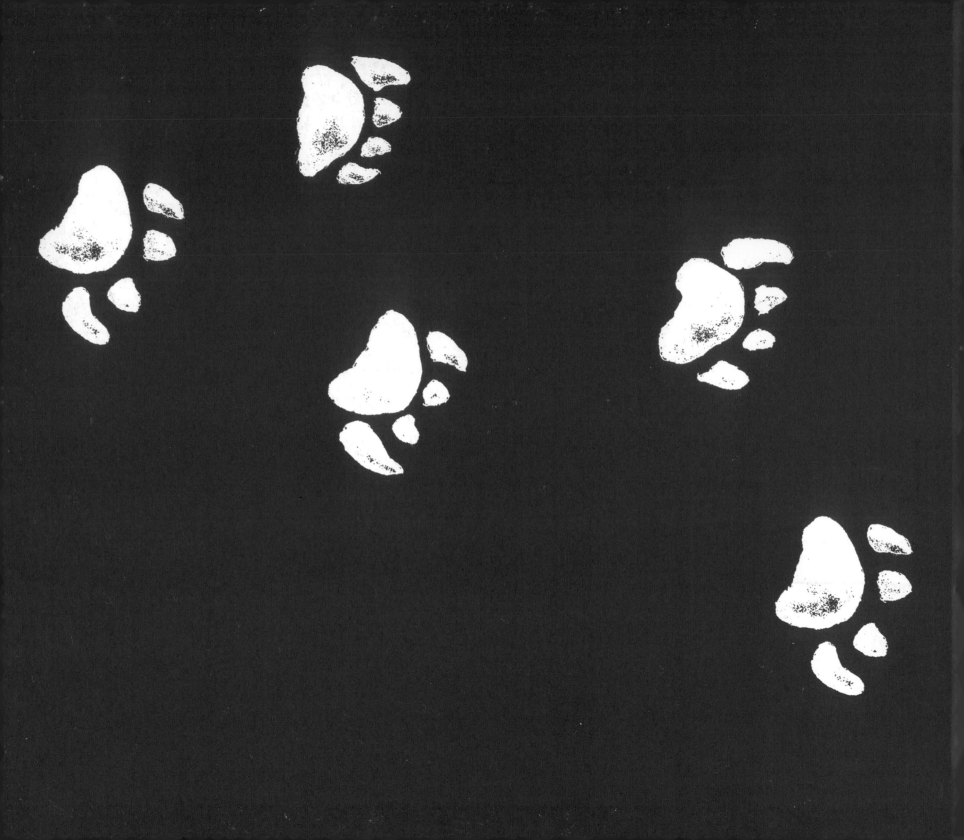